Sidney and the Hurricane

By Mark Booth

Illustrated by Patricia DeCosta

Designed by Daron Lowe

Published by
The Bermudian Publishing Company Limited
P.O. Box HM 283, Hamilton HM AX
Bermuda

Printed in Singapore

1995
First Edition
ISBN 976-8143-13-4

Sidney the Sailboat was having a lovely day with his owner Captain Haggard and their new friend, a young boy named Billy.

They had left the boat club early that morning, loaded with fishing rods, bait and enough food and drink for the whole day.

"I know just the spot for fishing not far from Mangrove Bay," Captain Haggard had boasted as they set off.

Actually, not one fish had been caught, but as they bobbed up and down on the clear blue water listening to the Captain tell stories of his adventures at sea, it really didn't seem to matter.

Now the sun was slowly starting to dip towards the west and it was time to raise Sidney's anchor and head for home.

A puff of wind filled Sidney's two white sails and off they went gliding across the water.

Billy watched contentedly as small wooded islands and houses with bright white roofs passed slowly by. As they moved along, he dragged his hand in the water. It felt cool and fresh. Then he noticed something.

"Captain, look! There's a small bridge straight ahead and I'm sure Sidney will not be able to get under it. Quick, turn around!"

Captain Haggard smiled. *"Don't worry lad, this is Somerset Bridge. They say it's the smallest drawbridge in the world. Just wait and see what happens."*

When they were closer, Billy saw a man waving to them from the bridge. Captain Haggard waved back. The man seemed to know what to do as he lifted a small plank of wood from the middle of the bridge, leaving a gap just large enough for Sidney's wooden mast to pass through.

Billy looked up as the bridge passed by, not far above his head.

Sidney always thought going through Somerset Bridge was such good fun.

Once on the other side, Sidney's sails were again pulled in and they were soon racing across the Great Sound, pushed along by a strong southerly breeze.

Before long, they were sailing past the city of Hamilton and getting near to the boat club.

"*Ready about!*" called Captain
Haggard, which Billy knew
meant they would soon change
direction, "*Lee ho!*" Billy let go of
one of the two ropes that held a
small sail called the jib and as
the Captain turned Sidney into
the wind, he pulled hard on the
other.

They were now heading straight for Sidney's mooring near the shoreline. *"Release the main sail!"* shouted the Captain. Billy immediately lowered Sidney's largest sail.

Sidney glided slowly to the big white buoy that marked his anchor.

Razor, a red motor boat that was watching, as usual decided to say something nasty.

"What a performance! First you go left, then you go right, just to get back to where you started. My engines take me in a straight line to wherever I want to go. It doesn't matter to me which way the wind is blowing."

"*You will never understand,*" replied Sidney. "*The wind is quiet and clean while your engines are loud and dirty.*"

Sidney wished his friend Rebecca, a lovely white and red sailboat was there to argue with Razor, but she was much bigger than Sidney and was away racing against other boats across the ocean.

Sidney was really looking forward to seeing her again and hearing about all her adventures.

Billy folded Sidney's sails and stored them in the cabin as he had been taught. He was washing the deck when he noticed Captain Haggard staring up at the sky with a worried look on his face. *"I don't like the look of it,"* the Captain mumbled to himself.

"Is something wrong Captain?" asked Billy. Captain Haggard pointed to the sky. *"Do you see those clouds? Well, the last time I saw a pattern like that, it was twenty years ago in the South China Sea, Two days later we were hit by a hurricane."*

"What is a hurricane?" asked Billy curiously.

"*It's the biggest storm that you will ever want to see,*" answered the Captain. "*The wind can blow so hard that you can't stand up without being blown over and the waves can become as big as a house. It's a terrifying sight. I think we had better turn the radio on and listen for any news.*"

Billy looked at the clouds again. They did look a little bit strange. He really hoped the Captain was wrong.

B ut it wasn't too long before Captain Haggard was indeed proved right.

"Attention all shipping. This is Harbour Radio. We have been advised of a hurricane-strength storm approaching from the south-west. The Hurricane has been named Emily and we expect to feel its effects within 24 hours. We advise all shipping to find a sheltered mooring. Please listen for further updates."

O ut at sea, Rebecca's radio had broken, and so she continued sailing, completely unaware that the hurricane was coming straight towards her.

The next day was very busy with all the boats in Hamilton Harbour being prepared for the hurricane's expected arrival. Some, like Razor, had extra ropes tied to them so that they would not be blown away from their moorings, while other were moved to more sheltered areas.

Captain Haggard and Billy moved Sidney to a place behind the boat club's concrete dock. *"You will be safer here Sidney,"* said Captain Haggard.

Sidney could just about see over the dock wall into the deep water of the Great Sound. The waves were certainly getting bigger, as the wind continued to grow stronger.

The news on the radio continued to report that Hurricane Emily was on its way.

"Attention all shipping. This is Harbour Radio, We are unable to contact the sail boat Rebecca. If you see her, please advise her captain of the serious situation."

Sidney could hardly believe it. Poor Rebecca was sailing straight into the hurricane. She was certain to sink.

Out at sea, the waves were very big, and Rebecca wished she was home with Sidney. She even missed Razor, if only a little.

Captain Haggard and Billy prepared Sidney for the arrival of the hurricane. The sky had turned very grey and branches on the trees started blowing around ferociously.

"Billy, I think it's time for you to go home now," said Captain Haggard.

"But, I want to stay with Sidney," pleaded Billy.

"No lad, the Captain always stays with his ship. You go home."

Billy, reluctantly left but promised to return as soon as it was safe.

The night passed slowly as everyone listened to news of Hurricane Emily and waited for its unwelcome arrival.

Sidney was pleased when morning finally arrived as it seemed slightly less frightening when he could see what was happening. Water crashed into the dock wall that protected him, while out in the harbour Razor looked nervously around as he was tossed up and down by each passing big wave.

The noise of the wind became deafening. Captain Haggard patted Sidney. *"This is it. Emily has arrived,"* he whispered.

At that moment, a large branch from a tree flew through the air carried by the wind as if it were light as a feather. The branch crashed into the side of the boat club.

Sidney could see other trees bending like twigs, with many of them breaking. Limestone slate, ripped from roofs in Hamilton, blew around like pieces of paper.

"**Jumping jellyfish!**" exclaimed Captain Haggard. Across the harbour the cruise ship Prince William had broken away from its moorings and was drifting out of control. In its path were some very scared-looking boats, including Razor.

Sidney and the Captain watched as three tug boats went to try and help the large cruise ship, but the force of the hurricane pushed her slowly but surely towards Razor.

Sidney and Razor had always argued, but Sidney now wished he could help the motor boat somehow.

Razor looked across the harbour in horror at the big ship moving towards him. The tugs were pushing with all their might to keep the cruise ship away, and clouds of black smoke from the ship's funnel showed its own engines were working as hard as they could. Still, the Prince William could not be stopped.

Meanwhile, out at sea Rebecca and her crew were completely exhausted.

Bravely she sailed on as wave after huge wave came crashing down onto her deck, while the deafening noise of the wind howled all around. Finally, she saw the familiar Gibbs Hill Lighthouse which meant they were nearly home at last.

However, her joy quickly turned to despair when she noticed a big wave coming towards her. It looked as high as a mountain. All Rebecca could do was close her eyes and wait for it to hit.

Suddenly, the trees stopped bending and it became strangely quiet. *"The hurricane must have passed,"* thought a relieved Sidney.

But Captain Haggard knew better: *"We are in the eye of the hurricane, the very centre of the storm. It will be like this for a little while, then the wind will start all over again."*

Razor looked up at the white hull of the Prince William towering above him. *"Any minute now, I'm going to be smashed to bits,"* he thought, trembling with fear. But then, the strong winds were gone and he watched, relieved, as the tugs hurriedly pushed the ship away to safety.

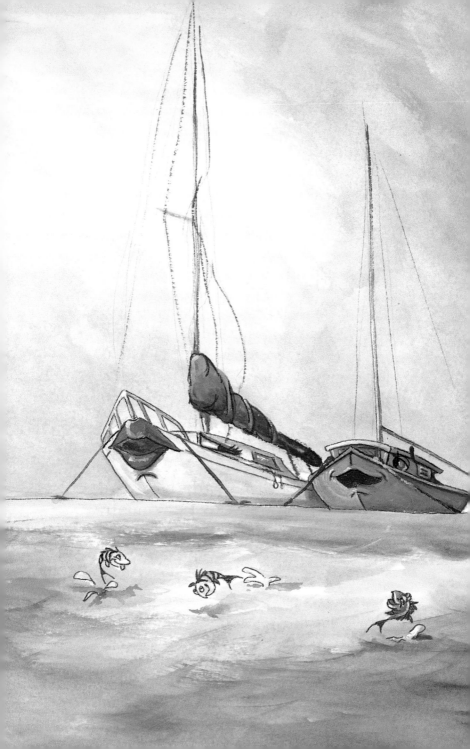

Sidney was glad Razor had been saved and was even happier when he noticed Rebecca sailing into the harbour, her sails ripped by the wind.

"Thank goodness you are safe," said a relieved Sidney. *"I am so pleased to be home,"* replied Rebecca. *"The waves were so big and the wind so strong. I thought I would never see you again."* Tears of joy filled her eyes.

As the Captain predicted, the wind soon started to blow again just as strongly as before. But all the boats were now safe, and as the day passed Hurricane Emily slowly moved away.

THE END

On the morning of September 25,
1987, Hurricane Emily
smashed into Bermuda.
High winds and towering waves
inflicted a huge amount of damage on
the Island's buildings,
trees and, of course, boats.

This story tells how Sidney the
Sailboat and his friends saw the
coming and going of
HURRICANE EMILY.

DEDICATIONS

To my children, Charlotte and Nicholas.
May all your dreams come true.
MARK BOOTH

To my inspiration, my charming son
Ryan. I will always love you, Ryan.
PATRICIA DeCOSTA

ISBN 976-8143-13-4